MW00901791

Fantastic Cities
Adult Coloring Book

Name   : ....

Phone   : ....

Copyright © 2021. All rights reserved

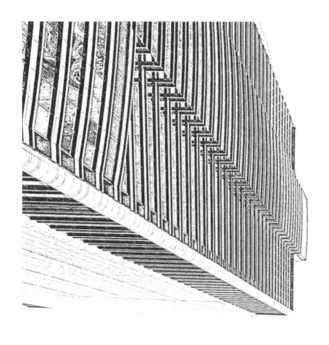
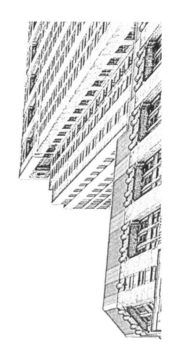
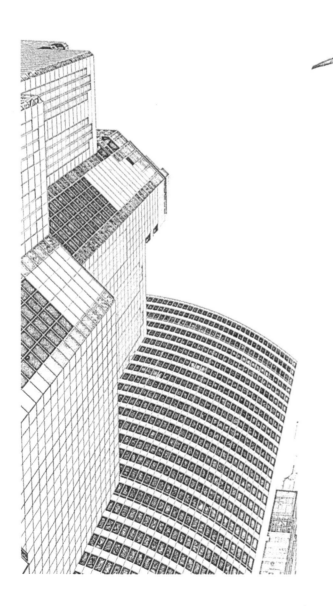
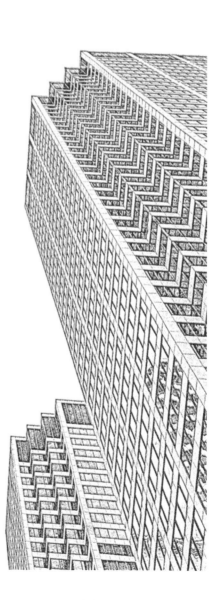

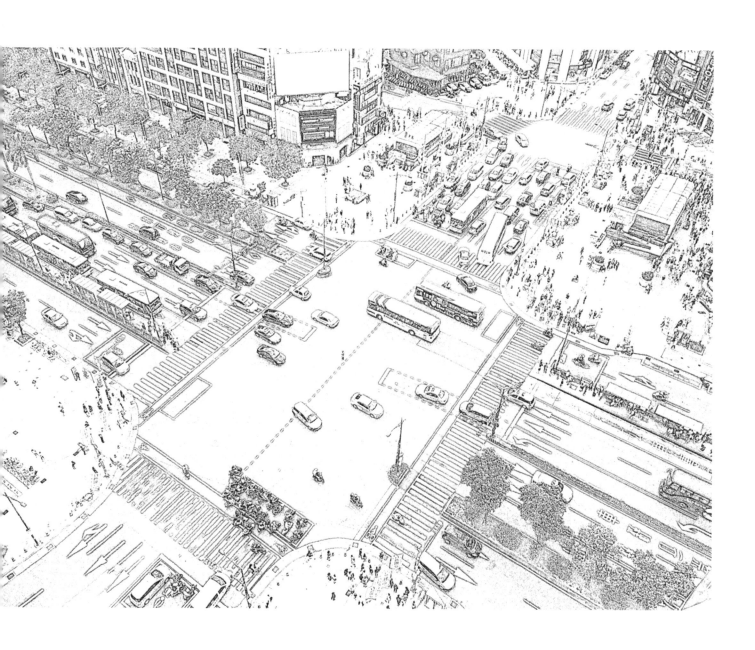

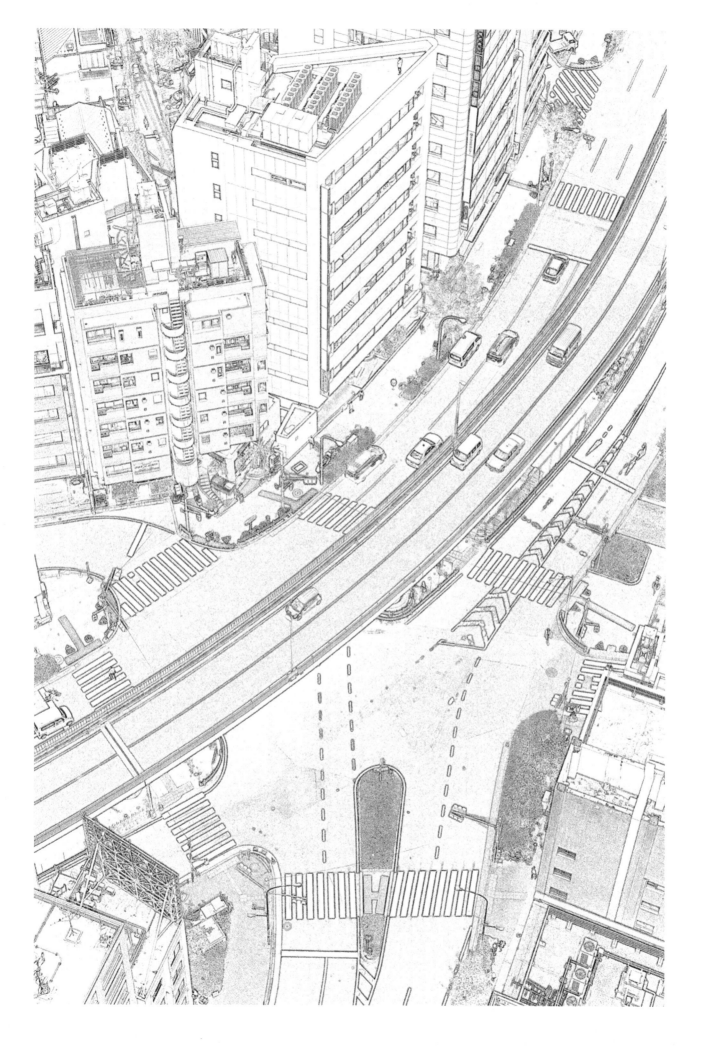

We create our books with love and great care. Your opinion will help us to improve this book and create new ones. We love to hear from you. Please, support us and leave a review!

Thank You!

Made in the USA
Monee, IL
02 March 2023

29016844R00037